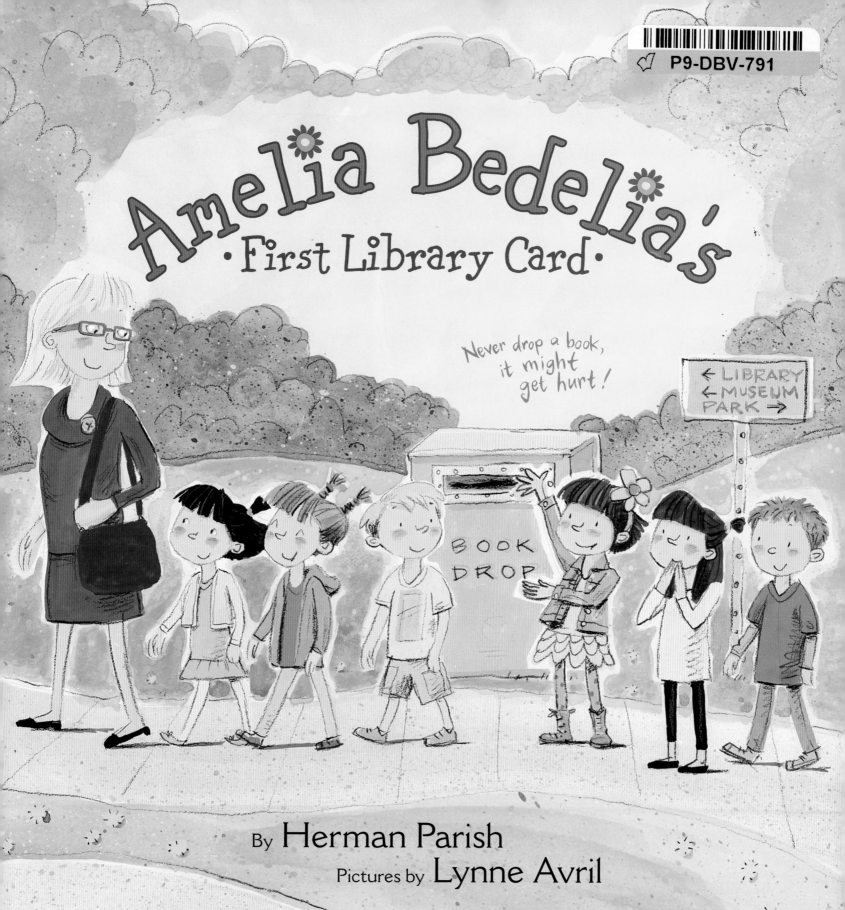

Amelia Bedelia's
• First Library Card •

Never drop a book, it might get hurt!

← LIBRARY
← MUSEUM
PARK →

BOOK DROP

By Herman Parish
Pictures by Lynne Avril

Greenwillow Books
An Imprint of HarperCollinsPublishers

For librarians everywhere . . .—H. P.

For Ginny, oh source of all knowledge—L. A.

The author thanks the children's librarians at the Princeton public library for their insights and advice.

Amelia Bedelia's First Library Card. Text copyright © 2013 by Herman S. Parish III. Illustrations copyright © 2013 by Lynne Avril.
Amelia Bedelia is a registered trademark of Peppermint Partners, LLC. All rights reserved. Printed in the U.S.A.
For information address HarperCollins Children's Books, a division of HarperCollins Publishers, 10 East 53rd Street, New York, NY 10022.
www.harpercollinschildrens.com
Gouache and black pencil were used to prepare the full-color art. The text type is Cantoria MT.

Library of Congress Cataloging-in-Publication Data: Parish, Herman. Amelia Bedelia's first library card /by Herman Parish ; pictures by Lynne Avril.
p. cm. "Greenwillow Books." ISBN 978-0-06-209512-1 (trade bdg.)—ISBN 978-0-06-209513-8 (lib. bdg.) [1. Libraries—Fiction. 2. Books and reading—Fiction.
3. Humorous stories.] I. Avril, Lynne, (date), ill. II. Title. PZ7.P2185Arl 2013 [E]—dc23 2012028700

13 14 15 16 17 LP 10 9 8 7 6 5 4 3 2 1 First Edition

 Greenwillow Books

Amelia Bedelia loved books, and she loved to read.
That's why she was so happy the day her teacher,
Miss Edwards, took the class to visit the town library.

"Welcome to the library!" said a lady in the lobby. "I am Mrs. Reilly, the children's librarian. We have lots of great things to show you. But first, one rule. There is no food or drink allowed in the library. We don't want any icky-sticky books, do we?"

"No!" shouted the class.

Amelia Bedelia quickly finished her juice box. She wasn't really supposed to be drinking it, anyway.

She looked around for a place to put it. The library really is great, she thought as she shoved her juice box into the handy trash can just for kids!

"Now, let me show you how to return a book," said Mrs. Reilly. "You just slip it in here, like this." She slid a book through the slot. "Let's go see where it went and what happens next."

Uh-oh, thought Amelia Bedelia.

Everyone followed Mrs. Reilly to see the bins that caught the
books. She reached into one bin and pulled out a crumpled juice
box. "We will check *this* in to the trash," she said, dropping it
into the wastepaper basket. "See why we don't like food or
drink in the library? This book is wet and sticky."

"Now come with me," said Mrs. Reilly.
"Let me introduce you to Thomas B.
at the circulation desk. He is
checking books in and checking
books out, too."

"Hey, kids!"
said Thomas B.
"Who wants to
check in a book?"

Everyone took a turn
with the book scanner—
beep! beep! beep!

The librarians showed the class how books are sorted onto carts, wheeled through the library, and put back exactly where they belong.

"We have books on every subject you can think of,"
said Mrs. Reilly, "from history to art to sports
to science. And there are lots of good stories
in the stacks, too!"

Amelia Bedelia didn't see any
stacks. She looked around for
something in piles, like hay or
pancakes. But all she could
see were shelves of books.

At last they arrived at the children's room.
"This is my favorite place," said Mrs. Reilly.
"Please make yourselves at home."

"Hey!" said Skip. "The
fish are afraid of me!"
"They can read,"
Amelia Bedelia said.
"Your shirt makes them
feel like lunch!"

Mrs. Reilly went to her desk and picked up a bundle of plastic cards. She removed the rubber band and put it on her wrist. "This is my librarian jewelry," she said, smiling. Then she gave the cards to Miss Edwards.

"Here is a library card for each one of you," said Miss Edwards. "Now you can check out books whenever you like."
The whole class cheered.

"Remember when we talked about how a library works, chickadees?" asked Miss Edwards. "The library shares these books with everyone in town."

"That's right," said Mrs. Reilly. "When you check one out, you are taking a turn with it. At our library, your turn lasts for three weeks."

Penny raised her hand. "What if you don't return your book on time?"

"Well, you can renew it, and get extra time," said Mrs. Reilly. "But if you keep it past the due date, you get a fine."

That sounded okay to Amelia Bedelia. Getting a "fine" was not as good as getting an "excellent," but it was not as bad as getting a "terrible."

"We have a few minutes before we head back to school," said Miss Edwards. "Please choose one book and then use your new library card to check it out."

"I'd like to check out this chapter book," said Dawn.
"Terrific," said Mrs. Reilly. "Let's try my finger test."
She opened Dawn's book to the first chapter. As she moved
her finger across the page, Dawn read each word out loud.
"Wonderful!" said Mrs. Reilly. "This is a perfect book for you.
Now, does anyone need help?"

Mrs. Reilly showed them where to find the chapter books and picture books.

She showed them where to find books about famous people and books about animals and books by their favorite authors.

Mrs. Reilly even showed them a special shelf of audiobooks. "These are for kids who like to read with their ears," she said. Amelia Bedelia decided that she wanted to learn to read with her eyes first.

With so many books, it was hard for Amelia Bedelia to choose just one. She held up her finger, shut her eyes, and twirled around and around. Aha! The winner of *her* finger test was on the top shelf! "Those are for the older kids," said Mrs. Reilly. "They're over your head."

"I know," said Amelia Bedelia. "That's why I need help."

"Come with me," said Mrs. Reilly. "I bet you'll like these books
better. They're exactly at your level."

Mrs. Reilly was right. Amelia Bedelia could reach them all. She
chose a book about cupcakes and got in line behind Teddy.

"Hey, Amelia Bedelia," said Teddy.
"Which one should I get?"
"Yahhhhhh!" yelled Amelia Bedelia.

Mrs. Reilly raised both eyebrows.
"Sorry," said Amelia Bedelia.
"I thought *Tyrannosaurus rex*
was going to bite off my nose!"

"I can't wait to read this to my
little brother," said Teddy.
He handed his other book to
Amelia Bedelia. "Here," he said.
"Check this one out."

Amelia Bedelia opened the book slowly and carefully. No teeth. No scales. No dinosaurs. This one was about clouds and the weather.

"Next!" said Thomas B.

"I'm just checking this out," said Amelia Bedelia.

"Looks interesting," said Thomas B. "May I see it, along with your library card?"

Amelia Bedelia handed him both. *Beep!*

"Here you go," said Thomas B. "It's due back in three weeks."

Oh, nooooooooooooo!

Amelia Bedelia was about to shout, "Wait! That's a mistake.
I didn't want the book about clouds. I want this book
about cupcakes!"
But just then, Miss Edwards called, "Time to go back to school!"

Amelia Bedelia was furious. On her way out, she glared at the book return slot. She felt like shoving the silly weather book in there right this minute! But then she wouldn't have a book to take home. This was supposed to be a great visit, but it had started out badly and ended worse!

Amelia Bedelia was still upset when she got home. She headed straight for her swing set and swung as high as she could, trying to kick every cloud out of the sky.

Then she lay down in the grass and looked up. As the clouds grew bigger and bigger, Amelia Bedelia imagined she could see all sorts of wonderful and happy things in them.

She took her library book
out of her backpack.
She had just found the
page that described the big,
stormy cloud above her when her mother
called, "Amelia Bedelia, Aunt Mary is here!"
"Yippee!" yelled Amelia Bedelia.

Aunt Mary brought Amelia Bedelia
a fancy purse—the perfect place
to carry her new library card.
"Thank you!" said Amelia Bedelia.
"This turned into a great day, after all!"
"You sound like you're on cloud nine,"
said Aunt Mary.
Amelia Bedelia couldn't wait
to look up cloud nine in her book.

BOOM

BOOM went a clap of thunder.
It began to pour. Her book!

"Oh, no!" said Amelia Bedelia. She ran to the rescue.

"I'll be right back."

"We can't go outside, young lady!" said her mother.

"It's too dangerous."

Another enormous *BOOM* rattled the windows.

The lightning and thunder and rain didn't let up. It stormed all afternoon and all through the night. Amelia Bedelia couldn't fall asleep for a long time. When she finally did, she dreamed about storm clouds filled with horrible, scary things.

The next morning was sunny, but Amelia Bedelia's library book was completely soaked. The pages looked all wrinkled, like her fingers did when she stayed in the bathtub too long.

Amelia Bedelia was too upset to eat her breakfast.

"Is something wrong?" her dad asked. "You look under the weather."

"I'm okay," she said. "But my library book was under the weather all night."

"Yipes," said her dad. "It's practically pulp!"

Amelia Bedelia let out a sob. She thought only orange juice had pulp.

"Oh, sweetie. Accidents happen," said her mom. "I'll take you to the library after school, and you can explain everything."

That afternoon, Amelia Bedelia and her mother went to the library.

"My, my," said Mrs. Reilly. "You really *did* read up a storm."

Amelia Bedelia's mother smiled and offered to replace the book.

"Thank you," said Mrs. Reilly. "Amelia Bedelia, I can tell that you love books as much as I do."

She put a rubber band on Amelia Bedelia's wrist. "Here is an official librarian's bracelet just for you."

"Thanks," said Amelia Bedelia. "I know you don't allow food in the library, but I brought you a cupcake to say I'm sorry."

"Hmmm," said Mrs. Reilly. "Can it pass my finger test?"
"Can you really read a cupcake?" Amelia Bedelia asked.

Mrs. Reilly took a swipe of frosting and tasted it.
"Yummm!" she said. "Amelia Bedelia, I'm glad you brought
this in for me to check out!"